Pterodactyl
Show and Tell

Written by Thad Krasnesky   Illustrated by Tanya Leonello

To my mother,
Margaret Krasnesky, career teacher
and lifetime Mom. -TK

To Chris, Ethan, and Erin,
with gratitude and love. -TL

Copyright © 2018 by Flashlight Press · Text copyright © 2018 by Thad Krasnesky
Illustrations copyright © 2018 by Flashlight Press
Illustrations by Tanya Leonello, based on drawings by David Parkins.

All rights reserved, including the right of reproduction, in whole or in part, in any form.
Printed in China. First Edition – October 2018

Cataloging-in-Publication details are available from the Library of Congress.

Hardcover 9781936261345, ePDF 9781936261567, EPUB 9781936261574, Mobipocket 9781936261581

Editor: Shari Dash Greenspan   Graphic Design: The Virtual Paintbrush
This book was typeset in Carrotflower. The title was typeset in Talk To Me.
The illustrations were rendered digitally.

Distributed by IPG · www.ipgbook.com

Flash
Light PRESS   Flashlight Press
              527 Empire Blvd. · Brooklyn, NY 11225
              www.FlashlightPress.com

No dinosaurs or children were harmed in the making of this book.

I brought my pterodactyl into school for show-and-tell.

He almost ate two kids
before we heard the morning bell.

My teacher had to make some minor changes in attendance,

and social studies looked more like
the War of Independence.

In reading we sat quietly and no one made a squeak.

At recess we enjoyed a lively game of hide-and-seek.

In math my pterodactyl learned that numbers can be fun.

At lunch my pterodactyl wondered which meal would be best.

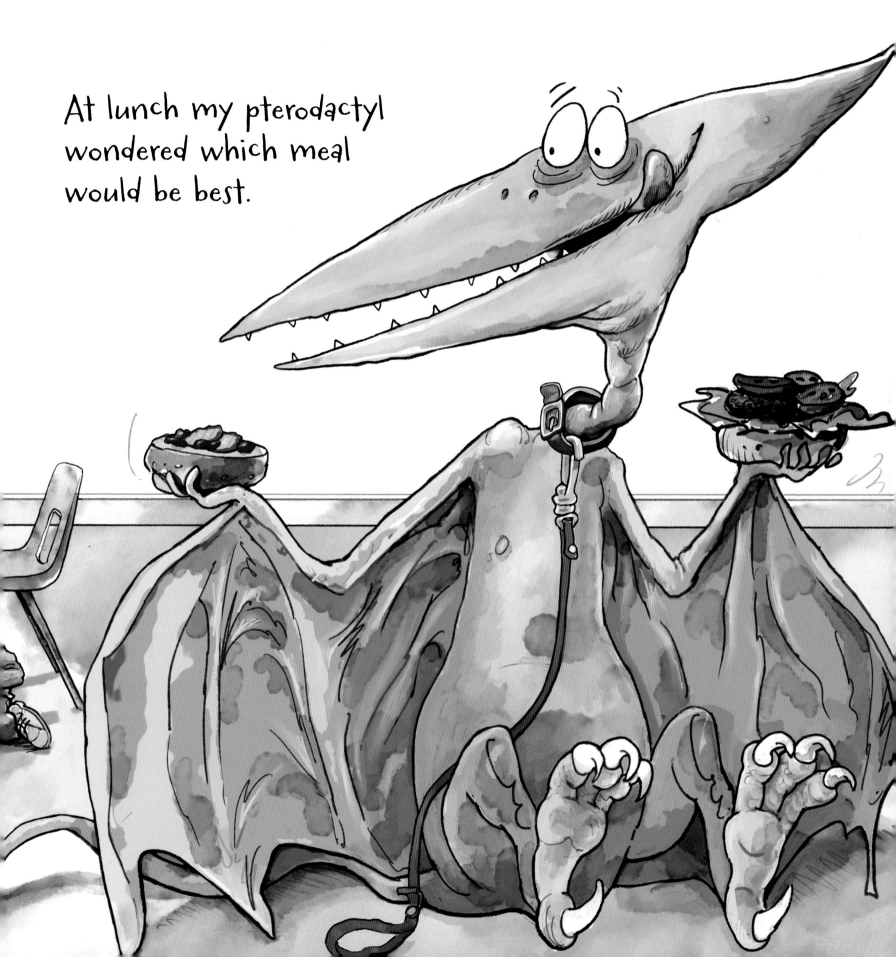

In science he experimented with a tasting test.

In art my pterodactyl made a prehistoric scene.

In health he showed us
how he keeps his teeth
so bright and clean.

In music class
my pterodactyl
kept a steady beat,

and in computer lab
he found a new way
to delete.

I never got a chance to
show-and-tell about my pet.
Perhaps that's why my teacher
looked a tiny bit upset.

She said I shouldn't bring
my pterodactyl anymore,
but since my class is gone
I've been promoted to grade four.

The fourth grade teacher made me
leave my pet out in the hall.

I guess those big fourth graders
don't do show-and-tell at all.